A Note to Parents

Eyewitness Readers is a compelling new program for beginning readers, designed in conjunction with leading literacy experts, including Dr. Linda Gambrell, President of the National Reading Conference and past board member of the International Reading Association.

Eyewitness has become the most trusted name in illustrated books, and this new series combines the highly visual *Eyewitness* approach with engaging, easy-to-read stories. Each *Eyewitness Reader* is guaranteed to capture a child's interest while developing his or her reading skills, general knowledge, and love of reading.

The four levels of *Eyewitness Readers* are aimed at different reading abilities, enabling you to choose the books that are exactly right for your children:

Level 1, for **Preschool to Grade 1**
Level 2, for **Grades 1 to 3**
Level 3, for **Grades 2 and 3**
Level 4, for **Grades 2 to 4**

The "normal" age at which a child begins to read can be anywhere from three to eight years old, so these levels are intended only as a general guideline.

No matter which level you select, you can be sure that you are helping your child learn to read, then read to learn!

A DK PUBLISHING BOOK
www.dk.com

Created by Leapfrog Press Ltd.

Project Editor Elizabeth Bacon
Art Editor Andrew Burgess

For DK Publishing
Senior Editor Linda Esposito
Senior Art Editor Diane Thistlethwaite
U.S. Editor Regina Kahney
Production Josie Alabaster
Picture Researcher Liz Moore
Illustrator Peter Dennis

Reading Consultant
Linda B. Gambrell, Ph.D.

First American Edition, 1999
2 4 6 8 10 9 7 5 3 1
Published in the United States by DK Publishing, Inc.
95 Madison Avenue, New York, New York 10016

Published in Great Britain by Dorling Kindersley Limited.

Eyewitness Readers™ is a trademark of
Dorling Kindersley Limited, London.

Library of Congress Cataloging-in-Publication Data
Clement-Davies, David, 1961-
  Trojan horse / by David Clement-Davies. -- 1st American ed.
    p.   cm. -- (Eyewitness readers. Level 4)
  Summary: A retelling of how the Greeks used a wooden horse to win
the ten-year-long Trojan War.
  ISBN 0-7894-4474-7 (hardcover). -- ISBN 0-7894-4475-5 (pbk.)
  1. Trojan War--Juvanile literature. 2. Mythology, Greek--Juvenile
literature. [1. Trojan War. 2. Mythology, Greek.] I. Title.
  II. Series.
BL793. T7C57 1999
398.2' 0938' 02--dc21   98-53380
                                                    CIP
                                                    AC

Color reproduction by Colourscan, Singapore
Printed and bound in Belgium by Proost

The publisher would like to thank the following
for their kind permission to reproduce their photographs:
Key: t=top, a=above, b=below, l=left, r=right, c=center

AKG UK Ltd: 4bl, 6tl; Ancient Art & Architecture: 8tl, 11br, 42tl /John King: 21tr
/Ronald Sheridan: 21br; Bridgeman Art Library: 12bl, 18tl, 25br, 37tc, 42bl, 46tlc;
Andrew Burgess: 40tl; Bruce Coleman Ltd: 17tr, 28tl; Dorling Kindersley Picture
Library: 7cr, 8bl, 10tl, b, 11tr, 13 all, 26b, 32bl, 34cl cla; /British Museum: 7tr, 24tl,
32tl, 33tr, 35cr, 42cl, 46tl; /Church's Ministry Among the Jews: 16tr, /Steve Gorton
39br; /Frank Greenaway: 39tr; /Bob Langrish/Mrs J Quinny: 28bl; /Natural History
Museum/Colin Keates: 39cr; /Natural History Museum/Harry Taylor:
46tlb; /Nick Nicholls: 13br, 18bl, 32tl, 32-33b, 33tr, 35cr, 37tr;
Clive Streeter: 37br; Mary Evans Picture Library: 4tl, 30tl;
/Garden Picture Library: 38tl; Sonia Halliday: 15br, 19tr,
44tl, 47tr; Robert Harding Picture Library: 5br, 12tl, 40bl, 46bl;
Michael Holford: 36bl; Images Colour Library: 15tr;
Jeff Moore: 27br; Science Photo Library: 24bl

The publisher would also like to thank
the London Lyceum of Greek Women for their kind help.

Contents

EYEWITNESS 👁 READERS

Level 4
GRADES 2-4

TROJAN HORSE

THE WORLD'S GREATEST ADVENTURE

Written by David Clement-Davies

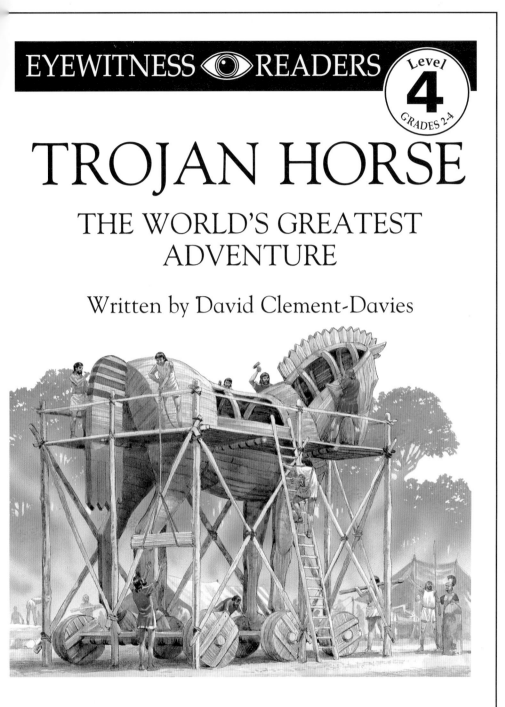

DK PUBLISHING, INC.
www.dk.com

Homer
Some historians think that Homer was blind. Others question if he lived at all.

Trojan mask
The ruins of ancient Troy were found in the late 19th century. Many treasures, including this gold mask, were dug up there.

Legends and heroes

About 2,700 years ago, Greece was one of the greatest civilizations in the world. The Greek writer Homer wrote two poems, *The Iliad* (ILL-ee-ad) and *The Odyssey* (ODD-uh-see). These poems told the story of a war between Greece and Troy 500 years before Homer lived. They were based on Greek history and legends.

Troy was a large walled city in what is now Turkey. Homer told how the Greeks tried to capture it for ten years, then thought up a clever scheme to invade the city by using a giant wooden horse.

The ancient Greeks prayed to many gods, called immortals. They built temples for their gods and offered them harvest fruits and animal sacrifices.

In the poems, the most important gods help start the war and interfere in the plan for the wooden horse.

EASTERN EUROPE

Black Sea

ITALY

•Mount Olympus
GREECE
Aegean Sea
•Mount Ida
Troy
Ithaca•
TURKEY

Sparta•
Mediterranean Sea

CRETE

—————— The Greeks' route to Troy

These include Zeus, king of the gods; his queen, Hera; and two of his daughters, Aphrodite and Athena. They discuss the war in heaven, then use magical powers to protect their favorite humans and punish those who make the gods angry.

The Iliad and *The Odyssey* are two of the world's best-known poems. This retelling includes some of the most exciting adventures in this magical tale of love and hate, power and revenge, gods and heroes.

Mount Olympus
(O-LIM-puss)
In Greek myth, this was the home of the gods, including: Zeus (ZOOS), Hera (HER-uh), Aphrodite (AFF-ro-DIE-tee), and Athena.

The golden apple

All day long the gods feasted on Mount Olympus. They drank from golden cups brimming with nectar and ate fabulous foods.

Heavenly drink
Nectar is the sweet liquid in flowers that bees make into honey. The gods drank nectar from golden cups.

Hera, queen of the gods, had invited all but one of the gods to the feast. She had not invited the goddess Spite, because Spite started arguments and created misery wherever she went.

But suddenly Spite appeared and stood glaring at the guests.

"Here is my gift to you," she cried, and threw a golden apple into the middle of the party.

On the apple were the words "FOR THE MOST BEAUTIFUL."

Hera snatched up the apple.

"I am queen of the gods," she said. "I must be the most beautiful. The apple is mine."

But Athena, the goddess of wisdom, darted forward.

"No, Hera," she said jealously. "The apple belongs to me."

Then Aphrodite sidled in between them.

"I am the goddess of love and beauty," she sighed. "Surely the apple is mine."

A quarrel broke out between the proud goddesses, though each was more beautiful than any woman on earth. The happy day was ruined.

Goddesses
Each goddess controlled a different aspect of human life and had a symbol to represent the aspect. Queen Hera's symbol was a peacock – a royal bird.

Athena
The goddess of wisdom and warfare was symbolized by a wise owl.

Aphrodite
The goddess of love was symbolized by a red rose.

Flock of sheep
Since ancient times, Greek shepherds have herded sheep and goats for milk, cheese, and wool.

Twin pipes
Pipes are like wooden flutes. Greek shepherds played a pair of pipes made from sycamore wood.

Zeus, king of the gods, grew tired of the goddesses' quarrelling. He sent them to see a shepherd named Paris, who lived on Mount Ida near the city of Troy. Paris was famous for his good judgment.

Paris sat playing his pipes in the morning sunlight when the goddesses appeared before him.

He was dumbstruck at the sight of the three dazzling immortals.

Hera placed the golden apple on the dewy grass.

"This apple is for the most beautiful goddess. Zeus commands you to choose which one of us deserves it," she said. "If you give it to me, I will give you as much power on earth as Zeus has in heaven."

Then bright-eyed Athena spoke: "If you give me the prize, I will make you the wisest man in the world and the winner of every battle."

Then Aphrodite smiled, and Paris was nearly blinded by her beauty.

"Paris, if you give me the prize you shall have Helen, a daughter of Zeus. She is as beautiful as I am."

Without a second thought, Paris took the apple and handed it to Aphrodite. As the goddesses vanished, Hera and Athena vowed to make Paris, their enemy, suffer.

Superwoman
According to Greek legend, Helen's father was Zeus and her mother was a human woman named Leda. Helen's beauty had a goddess-like power over people.

Paris and Helen

Soon after, King Priam of Troy decided to hold a sports contest in memory of a son who had died at birth. He sent his servants to Mount Ida to capture a bull for first prize.

Paris heard the servants talking. The thought of being champion of the king's games thrilled him. He left peaceful Ida and went down into the city of Troy.

The strong young shepherd showed his skill in every event.

Royal beast
Bulls were thought to be king of the beasts. They were often used as sports prizes.

Pentathletes
Like Paris, athletes today often compete in a pentathlon, a contest of five events.

He won two throwing contests and the jumping, wrestling, and running competitions, even beating the royal princes.

Hector, the eldest prince, drew his sword to kill the shepherd who dared challenge him. Just then, an old man threw himself at King Priam's feet.

"My lord!" he cried. "This is no ordinary shepherd. This is the beloved son in whose memory you are holding these games."

Priam was amazed. The old man continued, "Remember when your son was born? Your wife dreamed that he would cause the destruction of Troy. You ordered me to take the baby to Mount Ida and leave him to die. He was at the mercy of the bitter cold, but he survived. I have watched him grow up into a fine young man."

Priam was overjoyed that he had found his son again. He gave Paris his rightful place as a prince of Troy.

Wreath
Men honored the gods by holding sporting events. Winners were given a laurel wreath to wear. The laurel is the holy tree of the god Apollo.

Chilly peaks
The mountains near Troy reached up to 10,000 feet (3,048 meters) high. Wolves and other wild animals roamed the icy regions.

Ancient Sparta
The powerful city of Sparta was ruled by a king and queen. Spartan people excelled in arts and war.

Sailing ships
Homer called Greek ships "beaked" because they had long thin fronts, often decorated with birds' heads. The fronts could ram enemy ships.

Later that night, Paris woke up and saw Aphrodite shimmering before him. She whispered, "Helen is the queen of Sparta. Go and find her there, Paris. Remember, I will always protect you, for you gave the golden apple to me."

The next day Paris tied a silver picture of Aphrodite to his ship's mast, for he was about to make a voyage of love. He set sail across the glittering seas. When he arrived in Sparta and caught sight of Helen, his heart blazed with desire for her.

Paris brought greetings from Priam and sweet perfumes for Helen. Her husband, King Menelaus (men-uh-LAY-uss), welcomed Paris into his fine palace. His slaves bathed Paris and dressed him in a purple robe.

Then they led Paris to a chamber where his royal hosts were waiting. The feast looked delicious but Paris found it impossible to eat.

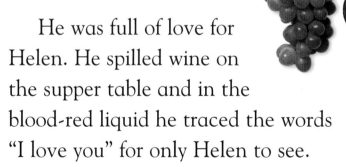

Olives

Goat's cheese

Bread with goat's cheese

Bread

Figs

Wine cup

Fish

Grapes

He was full of love for Helen. He spilled wine on the supper table and in the blood-red liquid he traced the words "I love you" for only Helen to see.

Helen's heart beat fast with excitement and fear. Paris watched her. He longed to be with her at any cost, even though she was the wife of Menelaus, noble king of Sparta.

Wine and dine
Fish, cheese, fruit, and wine were served at a feast. Meat was eaten only on religious occasions.

13

Night fell. Only Paris and Helen stayed awake, and they sat talking quietly. Now Aphrodite wove her powerful magic for Paris. She made Helen fall madly in love with him.

Paris took Helen's hand and led her out of the silent palace to his waiting ship. They set sail back to Troy, across the moonlit sea.

The goddess Hera still hated Paris for not giving her the apple. She sent wild storms to wreck the lovers' ship, but Aphrodite made sure that they reached Troy unharmed.

The Trojans gave their prince a joyful welcome home. Only the prophetess Cassandra, Priam's daughter, was unhappy to see Helen.

She warned the people that Helen would bring disaster on Troy, but none of the Trojans believed her.

Aphrodite's spell slowly wore off Helen. Alone in her chamber, the queen wept for what she had done.

Danger at sea
The Aegean (i-GEE-an) Sea between Sparta in Greece and Troy in Turkey is often stormy.

Prophets
People who predicted the future were called prophets (PROFF-itts). Greeks visited temples where they asked for a prophecy from a priest, who was a prophet.

When the sun rose over Sparta the next day, Menelaus stormed through his palace. He tore Paris's purple robe in two and roared to the heavens, "I call on you gods to help me get revenge on that traitor Paris!"

Athena heard his prayer and smiled. She was ready to help him.

Menelaus needed men to sail to Troy with him and win back Helen. He sent messengers to the kings and princes of Greece.

Each ruler had sworn an oath to protect Helen in times of danger.

From every island and mountaintop kings and princes journeyed to Sparta with soldiers.

Two great warriors joined the Greek army: Odysseus (oh-DISS-ee-us), king of Ithaca, and Achilles (a-KILL-eez), the son of a goddess.

A magnificent fleet of one thousand and thirteen ships set sail for Troy. The sun god Apollo blew a gentle wind to speed their voyage and told dolphins to play and leap above the sparkling waves.

Dolphins
Sailors believed that Apollo commanded the dolphins. If his dolphins followed them, they were safe.

Fine fast fleets
Greek warships were light and fast. Each had a big linen sail and was rowed by 50 oarsmen.

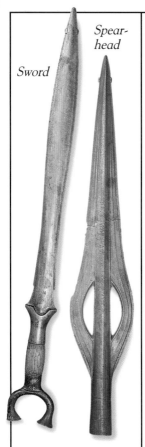

Sword

Spear-head

War weapons
Soldiers carried bronze weapons such as swords and spears. They wore bronze helmets which were embossed, or decorated.

Helmet

The war begins

The ships were blown through black storms one minute, then they sailed under blue skies the next, for the gods were arguing. Zeus sent down thunder and lightning to please Aphrodite. Then Apollo blew the storm clouds away and calmed the winds, which delighted Athena.

Three weeks later the fleet landed on the shores of Troy. The army was immediately attacked by an angry swarm of Trojans. Achilles led the Greeks into the first battle. Both sides fought ferociously. Swords sparked and clashed in the midday sun.

Achilles fought with such skill that the Trojans lost courage and fled back inside the walls of Troy. They barred the heavy city gates.

The Greek army sent Odysseus and Menelaus to talk to Priam and demand Helen's return. The old king listened to the noble leaders.

But the Trojan people were in no mood for peace and they turned violently on Odysseus and Menelaus. The two heroes only just escaped. Furious, the Greeks declared war.

On the plain outside the city and along the shore where their ships were anchored, the Greeks put up their tents. That night the shore was lit with hundreds of flickering campfires.

Plain of Troy
The flat plain between Troy and the sea was about 1.6 miles (2.5 kilometers) wide.

The Trojans stayed safe behind
their high city walls, and try as they
might, the Greeks could not capture
the city. They gave up trying to
smash down the walls.
Instead, they surrounded
Troy and attacked the
nearby villages. The siege
continued for days and
months and then years.
In the tenth year, a
terrible argument broke
out between Achilles
and a noble Greek
commander. They
fought bitterly over
who should own a
beautiful slave girl.
"I'll never fight the
Trojans for you again!"
Achilles swore angrily
to the commander,
"even if you beg me on
your knees to help you!"

Achilles stormed back to his tent and ripped off his armor in a rage.

It was up to Odysseus to rally the weary Greeks.

"Come, brave warriors, we can still win Helen and conquer Troy without Achilles," he cried. "Ten long years have passed and now it is time for victory!"

The soldiers cheered and took up their weapons. They marched on to the great plain and waited.

The Trojans saw that Achilles was not leading his army. They no longer had to fear him! Their great warrior, Hector, led his charioteers out of the city. Dust clouds flew up as horses' hooves and chariot wheels thundered across the dark plain of Troy.

Yurt
Warriors' tents were probably made of animal skins. Similar tents, called yurts, are found today in parts of Asia.

Chariots
Chariots were two-wheeled, horse-drawn vehicles, used to carry army leaders to the front lines.

A duel for peace

The two armies met on the battle plain. Hector and his Trojans advanced with war cries, while the Greeks moved forward in grim silence to meet their enemy.

The armies were on the brink of battle when Paris rode out from the Trojan ranks and faced the Greeks.

"I challenge any Greek to a duel, man to man!" he shouted boldly.

"The winner shall have Helen and this long war will end."

Menelaus, hungry for revenge, leaped down from his bronze chariot.

"Paris, you miserable thief!" he cried. "I will fight you!"

Paris was terrified that his arch-rival had taken up the challenge. Trembling, he backed away.

Hector persuaded his cowardly brother to fight.

"Paris, for once act like an honorable man. Remember, lovely Helen will be in the high tower watching you. Fight for her like a hero."

So Paris and Menelaus took up their weapons. First Paris hurled his spear at Menelaus, but he missed. Menelaus sprang toward Paris, grabbed him by the throat and dragged him toward the Greek lines.

Athena hovered above Menelaus. Her steely eyes flashed with triumph.

At that moment Aphrodite flew down, hid her beloved Paris in a mist, and spirited him away from the battlefield.

But Menelaus had won the duel and peace was declared at last.

Wine cup
The gods were served nectar by a male or female servant called a cupbearer.

God speed
A meteor is a rock-like object that shoots from outer space through the sky. Several other gods besides Athena were said to travel as forces of nature. For example, Zeus traveled as a thunderbolt.

On Mount Olympus, Hera and Athena stood glaring at Zeus, who was sipping red nectar.

"Well," Zeus mocked the two angry goddesses, "Aphrodite is working hard to protect her Trojan prince. What are you two doing for the Greeks? Perhaps you are both happy now that peace has been declared between the two armies?"

Hera stamped her foot in rage and yelled at her husband, "How dare you say that! This war should go on until the Greeks conquer Troy! Zeus, let Athena ruin the peace between the Greeks and the Trojans!"

There was silence. Then Zeus sighed, "Very well. Send my warrior-child to stir up the war again."

Athena dived from heaven, disguised as a blazing meteor.

Her fiery spirit seized the heart of a Trojan soldier and made him long to be a hero by killing a Greek leader.

"Forget peace," he thought, "I will fight for my city and my king."

Menelaus stood near the gates of Troy. The young Trojan crept up behind him, his hand on his sword. But Menelaus swung around just in time, and the cowardly Trojan fled.

The precious peace was broken. The furious Greek army turned on the Trojans, and battle cries echoed across the plain once more.

Homer's description of battles are a mixture of what happened in his own and in earlier times. In his day, soldiers fought in long blocks. Earlier, soldiers were less rigidly organized and often fought hand-to-hand.

Shields were made from layers of animal skin, or hide, edged in bronze.

Hector, Trojan hero

That night, outside the royal palace,
Hector stood surrounded by his soldiers.
They were pleading with him: "Hector,
how can we force back the angry
Greeks? Show us how to fight them!"

Hector was silent. He looked up
at the stars. Then he left his men and
went inside the palace to see his family.

He threw off his red cloak and put
on his armor. His wife looked at him
with fear in her dark eyes.
She was certain he was
going to die in battle.

Hector knelt down
to kiss his son, but the
baby was terrified of
his father's shining
helmet with its horns
and horsehair plume.

Hector laughed
and took off the
helmet. He lifted his
son high and said,

"Little one, as lovely as a star, one day you will be a brave Trojan hero!" Kissing his wife, Hector told her, "The gods give me no choice. I must fight to the death, my love."

In battle, Hector fought so bravely that the Greeks fled in terror toward the shore. Then the Trojans started to set fire to the Greek ships.

Without Achilles the Greeks were lost. Patroclus, Achilles' best friend and cousin, raced to the hero's tent.

"Achilles, we are in real danger! Let me wear your armor!" he begged. "I will fool the Trojans into thinking I am you. They will retreat in panic."

Achilles agreed, but warned him, "Patroclus, do not try to capture Troy alone. If you do, you will anger Apollo, who now loves the Trojans!"

Trojan torch
Soldiers used burning torches to set fire to enemy ships. The light warships were made of quick-burning wood.

Vulture
People believed gods could change into different forms. Warlike Athena turned into this bird often seen near places of battle.

Chariot horse
The warriors' chariot horses were probably similar to the modern Caspian horse.

Dressed as Achilles, Patroclus led the Greek army out to fight the Trojans. Athena disguised herself as a vulture, and watched from the top of a tall pine tree. Apollo stood on the walls of Troy, robed in sunlight.

When the Trojans saw Patroclus, their hearts sank. They thought Achilles had returned to fight! They stumbled over one another in terror as they tried to escape his spear.

Many Trojan heroes were killed, and the rest scattered in front of Patroclus. Even mighty Hector leaped into his chariot and wheeled it around, shouting to the Trojans to run for the gates of Troy.

But Patroclus was far too bold. He forgot Achilles' warning and raced toward Troy on his own.

Apollo saw the hero trying to scale the city walls. The furious god flung him down onto his chariot.

Then Apollo shot a ray of sun
to blind Patroclus's horse. It reared
in fright and Patroclus tumbled from
his chariot. His helmet flew from his
head and his spear broke into pieces.

Hector shouted to the Trojans,
"It was a trick! He is not Achilles!"

As Patroclus tried to crawl away,
Hector killed him with a single blow.
He stripped Achilles' armor from the
dead body. Then, with a war cry,
Hector led the Trojan soldiers back
into the heat of battle.

Sun god
Apollo was the
gods' archer.
He used rays of
the sun as
golden arrows.
He is often
shown riding a
golden chariot
across the sky.

Hard hitter
The blacksmith of the gods was also the god of fire. He forged fine metal objects for the gods, such as shoes for Apollo's chariot horses.

River Styx
In Greek legend the River Styx (STICKS) divided the land of the living from Hades (HAY-dees), the kingdom of the dead.

Death of the heroes

A messenger ran and told Achilles that Hector had killed Patroclus and taken his armor. Achilles cried out so loudly that his mother, the sea goddess Thetis, heard him from her sea cave and sped to her son's side.

"Mother," he wept, "help me to avenge my beloved friend's death!"

That night on Mount Olympus, Thetis asked the blacksmith of the gods to make her son a brand-new suit of armor. The god set to work, surrounded by fire and steam.

In the pale dawn, Thetis, cloaked in silvery mist, carried a gleaming helmet and shield to Achilles.

"My son," Thetis whispered, "listen carefully. When you were a baby I dipped you in the River Styx whose waters give everlasting life to those who touch them.

"But your heel stayed dry. If your heel is wounded you will die."

Achilles put on the golden
helmet and took the mighty shield.
He went to the walls of Troy and
called on Hector to fight him.

The air rang with the sound of
clashing swords and spears. Hector
fought well, but try as he might,
he could not pierce Achilles'
magical armor. At last Achilles
thrust his long spear into
Hector's neck.

Then Achilles
tore off Hector's
armor and tied
the hero's body
to the back of his
golden chariot.

Three times
Achilles circled
Troy in his chariot,
while old King Priam
and the Trojans
watched in horror
from the city walls.

Plain cruelty
The bodies
of those who
died in battle
were treated
with respect.
Achilles' cruelty
was shocking.

Oil flask

Last respects
A hero's body was covered in oil and wrapped in cloth before burning.

Buried treasure
Most people were buried with their treasures.

Day after day Achilles dragged Hector's broken body around the city walls behind his chariot. He refused to return the dead hero to the grieving Priam.

The gods grew angry, because the body of a hero must be burned if his soul is to find rest. Even Thetis could not reason with her stubborn son.

One night King Priam visited Achilles in his tent and begged for his son's body. Priam's grief touched Achilles' heart. He agreed to return Hector's body but only in exchange for Hector's weight in gold.

Achilles built a giant pair of scales outside Troy. On one side the Greeks laid Hector's body. On the other side the Trojans placed all of Priam's gold. But Hector's body was still heavier than the treasure.

Cassandra, Hector's sister, leaned out from the high walls of Troy and took off her golden bracelet. She dropped it onto the gold. It tipped the balance. The body rose as the gold sank to the ground.

The Trojans lifted the body over the walls and built a funeral pyre.

Old gold
Ancient kings collected gold objects and money. Coins were introduced into ancient Greece in about 700 BC from Turkey.

Procession
A hero's funeral was a major event. Mourners, dressed in black, carried the body to the funeral pyre, where the body was burned. The women cut their hair as a sign of respect.

Hemlock leaves and flower

Poison arrow
Arrows were dipped in powerful poisons such as the juices of the hemlock plant. This caused a slow and very painful death.

The terrible siege went on and on. Achilles still wore his wonderful armor and no one could beat him.

But one day the warrior made a foolish boast on the battle plain.

"Look how strong I am," he cried. "I could even beat the gods!"

The god Apollo was looking down from Mount Olympus.

"It is time to punish Achilles; his vanity insults the gods," he thought.

Paris had also seen Achilles. He put a poisoned arrow to his bow, took aim, and fired from the walls.

Apollo turned the wind and blew the arrow straight toward Achilles' foot. The arrow pierced the hero's heel, the only weak part of his body. He gasped and fell. The arrow's deadly poison flowed through his strong veins. Slowly, and in terrible pain, the mighty Greek warrior died.

The Greeks could not believe that their great Achilles was dead.

They burned his body in front of the city. Thetis, heartbroken, carried her son's soul up to heaven.

Paris bragged of his skill in killing the hero, but he grew careless too. One day a Greek archer spotted Paris on the city walls and shot three poisoned arrows at him, fatally wounding him. Paris died, but both armies had to fight to the end.

Medical model
A part of your heel that is easily injured is called the Achilles tendon, after the ancient Greek hero's fatal weak spot.

Slaves
Greek society
depended on
slaves, people
who had no
freedom. Slaves
were put to
work as miners,
servants, and
teachers.

Could the Greeks conquer Troy now that Achilles was dead?

Odysseus, the cleverest of all the Greeks, had a brilliant idea. But first he wanted to spy on the Trojans and find out everything about their city.

He disguised himself as a runaway slave, then slipped through Troy's gates into the wide streets.

Near Priam's palace he mingled with the crowds and watched the Trojan guards on the city walls. Helen caught sight of him from the palace gateway.

Her heart leaped for joy when she recognized brave Odysseus. She waved to him to come into the palace.

This is part of a palace of ancient Greece. Priam's palace in Troy may have looked the same.

Helen led him to her private chamber. She whispered to him, "Odysseus, I am a prisoner here. Hector was my only friend and now he is dead. And his poor father, who is kind to me, still weeps. I do not miss Paris, but I mourn our great Achilles!"

Helen showed Odysseus the loom where every day she sat alone and wove pictures of the war and of her long-lost homeland of Sparta.

The pictures on the beautiful purple cloth reminded Odysseus of the family he had left in Ithaca and, for a while, he was sad. Then he spoke:

"Listen, dear Helen, I know how we can win this war and take you back to Menelaus and your country."

He told her his plan and swore her to secrecy. Helen gladly told him all she knew about the city. Then she bathed him and brought him wine.

Much later, Odysseus left her and crept silently out of Troy.

Looms
Every Greek woman could make cloth. Mothers taught their daughters how to spin wool and weave it on a loom.

Bath oil
Greek house guests were rubbed with olive oil and perfume after taking a bath.

Timber!
Pine trees can grow very tall in the wild. They have always been valued for their timber.

The wooden horse

The next day at the Greek camp, while a flame-red sun was rising, the leaders listened to Odysseus's plan. They all agreed it was excellent.

Odysseus took a ship builder and two other men to help him cut down fifty giant pine trees in the forest.

The Greeks used some of the trees to build a high wall on the plain. Hidden from sight behind the wall, they set to work.

They built a giant wooden horse, so big that thirty men could hide in the hollow middle.

They worked fast and by evening the horse was ready. Its mane and tail were painted purple and gold, and its eyes sparkled with purple gems. Under its legs were huge wooden wheels. It was a work fit for the gods!

That night Odysseus led thirty of his best warriors up a ladder into the horse's hollow stomach and pulled the big trap door shut behind them.

Odysseus's cousin, Sinon, disguised himself as a beggar and skulked in the shadows by the horse.

Then the Greeks took down the wall, packed everything into their ships, and sailed out of sight behind a nearby island.

That night the Greeks were full of new hope as they waited on the quiet waters for morning to come.

Tide dye
The Greeks used the ink from large sea snails to make a deep purple dye or paint.

Gemstones
The Greeks may have used amethysts (AM-uh-thists) for the horse's eyes.

Gold leaf
Very thin gold, called gold leaf, was used for painting.

Greek writing
The Greek alphabet was created over 2,800 years ago. The Trojans wrote and read in Greek.

Gift tokens
Gifts were often offered to the gods in thanks. Today, people still leave small tokens in church as a way of thanking God.

The next day Priam looked out from Troy's battered towers. The Greeks had vanished! On the calm sea there wasn't a ship in sight. All they could see on the plain of Troy was a mighty wooden horse.

The Trojans were overjoyed. They threw open the city gates and ran up to the strange horse. They crowded around it excitedly and read the gold writing on its side: "FOR THEIR RETURN HOME THE GREEKS OFFER THIS TO THE GODDESS ATHENA."

Sinon pushed his way through the crowd and spoke to the Trojans.

"The gods told the Greeks that they should offer Athena this gift and sail home," he lied. "But the gods said that it must be left outside Troy. Once the horse enters the city no one can ever conquer Troy!"

The Trojans were delighted and immediately began to pull the tall magical gift toward Troy.

40

"No!" cried Cassandra in terror. "The wooden horse is a trick!"

But no one listened to her. The Trojans rolled the giant wooden horse through the gates of Troy.

The people covered the horse in beautiful flowers. All day they drank wine and danced for joy.

"Peace has come and we have won!" they sang.

The Trojans fell asleep believing they were safe forever.

Festive flowers During Greek celebrations, people wore chains of roses and scattered rose petals.

That night the goddess Aphrodite took pity on the Trojans. She cast a spell over Helen, who left her chamber and led a sleepy Trojan soldier to the horse.

"What if there are Greeks hiding inside it?" asked Helen dreamily.

Then she called gently to each of the warriors inside the horse. Every time she spoke her sweet, enchanted voice sounded like their beloved wives and children.

It was almost more than the heroes could bear. Tears poured down their cheeks and they wanted to cry out to their loved ones.

Suddenly one of the men started to answer Helen's call.

Odysseus clapped his hand over the warrior's mouth so that he could not give them away.

Inside the dark belly of the wooden horse, the heroes kept as silent and still as statues.

"There's no one there," yawned the Trojan soldier at last, shaking his head. He and Helen went back to the palace to sleep.

Meanwhile, Sinon lit a fiery beacon by the city walls. From their ships the Greeks saw the red glow in the starry night sky. It was the signal they had been waiting for.

Bright light
Beacons were lit as signals for help or as a warning. Sometimes, at night or in fog, the fires were lit at different points along coastlines to guide ships past dangerous rocks.

The fall of Troy

The night was deathly quiet as the Greek army crept up the beach to the city gates, guided by the flickering signal.

Giant gateway
The gates of cities such as Troy were up to 26 feet (8 meters) high. Troy's main gate, which the Greeks may have stormed, was the Scaean (SEE-an) gate.

Inside the wooden horse the heroes lifted the great trap door and let down the ladder.

Odysseus led the quickest men across the courtyard to the gates of Troy. They killed the drunken lookouts and, using all their strength, heaved the gates open.

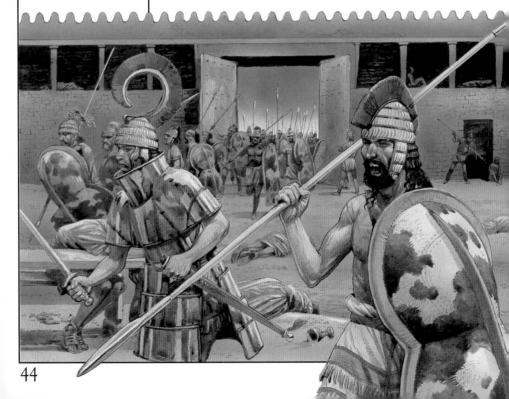

Outside, the Greeks helped push open Troy's mighty gates. The men streamed into the undefended city.

The sleeping Trojans were awakened by the noise. They cried out in terror, but they were doomed.

Look out!
Troy had tall sturdy towers near the gates, manned by lookouts. The lookouts should have seen the Greeks approaching and alerted the other soldiers to defend the city.

The Greeks rushed everywhere, filled with ten years of anger. They killed every Trojan man in sight and set fire to everything they could. They beheaded King Priam and made Cassandra and Hector's wife and son their prisoners.

Screams rang out as the Greeks dragged all the Trojan women and children to the Greek ships.

Troy's lofty towers and high walls burned to the ground. The palace treasures were stolen and every house was looted.

Soon the city streets were flowing with Trojan blood.

At last, Menelaus and his beautiful wife were reunited. Helen wept: "So many have died because of me!"

"But we have won you back, my treasure," Menelaus said gently. "Thanks to Odysseus and the wooden horse, we have conquered the city of Troy!"

After ten years of war, the Greek heroes set sail for home. The wind filled their ships' sails and carried them back across the rippling sea.

The gods looked down from Mount Olympus and plotted new adventures for the heroes.

Modern horse
In the modern city of Troy children can climb inside a model of the wooden horse.

Glossary

Avenge
The act of inflicting punishment on a person or people in return for harm or injury done to another party.

Beacon
(BEE-con)
A fire, light, or other signal used to guide or warn ships and aircraft.

Chariot
A two-wheeled open cart that is drawn by horses. The chariot was used in ancient times to carry soldiers.

Charioteer
The person who rides a chariot is called a charioteer.

Civilization
A society which has a written language, arts, science, and politics. The ancient Greek civilization was one of the greatest in world history.

Immortal
An immortal is someone who never dies. The Greek gods were immortal and could give people immortality, or everlasting life.

Legend
A famous story based on true events, but mostly made up by storytellers.

Lookout
A person responsible for keeping watch against danger.

Loom
A machine for weaving wool, cottons, or silk into thick or fine cloth.

Nectar
(NECK-ter)
A sweet liquid in many flowers that bees make into honey. Nectar was the drink of the gods. They ate food called ambrosia, which was nectar mixed with pollen, also from flowers.

Noble
Having or showing a brave and kind character. Also, a person of high rank.

Oath
A statement in which a person swears that he or she will speak the truth or keep a promise.

Pentathlon
A contest in which athletes take part in five track and field events. These events include running races, the long jump, and throwing.

Plume
A large, fluffy feather used to decorate a hat or a helmet. A Greek soldier's helmet had a plume made of horsehair, not feathers.

Prophecy
(PROFF-uh-see)
Something that a person says will happen in the future. In ancient Greece, even people who were not priests could make a prophecy.

Prophetess
A female who makes a prophecy.

Pyre
(PIRE)
A large heap or pile of wood on which a body is placed for burning in a funeral ceremony.

Revenge
The act of doing harm in return for harm or evil that has been done.

Rival
A person who competes with another for the same object. An arch-rival is a person who most wants what another has.

Sacrifice
To kill a person or animal in a ceremony because of a belief that it will please a god.

Siege
The act of surrounding a city by an enemy army that is trying to capture it.

Temple
A building where people pray to God or gods.

EYEWITNESS ◉ READERS

Level 1 *Beginning to Read*
A Day at Greenhill Farm
Truck Trouble
Tale of a Tadpole
Surprise Puppy!
Duckling Days
A Day at Seagull Beach

Level 2 *Beginning to Read Alone*
Dinosaur Dinners
Fire Fighter!
Bugs! Bugs! Bugs!
Slinky, Scaly Snakes!
Animal Hospital
The Little Ballerina

Level 3 *Reading Alone*
Spacebusters
Beastly Tales
Shark Attack!
Titanic
Invaders from Outer Space
Movie Magic

Level 4 *Proficient Readers*
Days of the Knights
Volcanoes
Secrets of the Mummies
Pirates!
Horse Heroes
The Trojan Horse